FIRST FAIRY TALES

Cinderella

For Natalie - *MM*
For Eve - *PN*

Series reading consultant: Prue Goodwin,
Reading and Language Information Centre,
University of Reading

Orchard Books
96 Leonard Street, London EC2A 4XD
Orchard Books Australia
32/45-51 Huntley Street, Alexandria, NSW 2015
This text was first published in Great Britain in the form
of a gift collection called *First Fairy Tales*,
illustrated by Selina Young, in 1994
This edition first published in Great Britain in hardback in 2002
First paperback publication 2003
Text © Margaret Mayo 2002
Illustrations © Philip Norman 2002
The rights of Margaret Mayo to be identified as the author and
Philip Norman to be identified as the illustrator have been
asserted by them in accordance with the
Copyright, Designs and Patents Act, 1988.
A CIP catalogue record for this book is available from the British Library
ISBN 1 84121 138 9 (hardback)
ISBN 1 84121 150 8 (paperback)
1 3 5 7 9 10 8 6 4 2 (hardback)
1 3 5 7 9 10 8 6 4 2 (paperback)
Printed in Hong Kong, China

FIRST FAIRY TALES
Cinderella

Margaret Mayo ⭐ Philip Norman

ORCHARD BOOKS

Once upon a time, there was a
beautiful girl called Cinderella.
She had two ugly stepsisters who
made her do all the work.

She had to sweep the floors,
cook the food and wash the dishes,
while they dressed up and went
to parties.

One day, a royal invitation arrived at Cinderella's house. The king's only son was going to have a grand ball, and the three girls were invited.

Cinderella knew she wouldn't
be allowed to go to the ball. But
the ugly sisters were excited. They
couldn't talk about anything else.

When the day of the ball came,
poor Cinderella had to rush about.

She fixed their hair, helped
them put on their new dresses,
and arranged their jewels, just so!

As soon as they had gone, Cinderella sat down by the fire, and she said, "I wish I could go to the ball!"

Then – *WHOOSH!* Beside her
stood a lady holding a silver wand.

"Cinderella," she said, "I am
your fairy godmother, and you
shall go to the ball!

But, first, bring me a pumpkin
from the garden,

six mice from the
mouse-traps,

a whiskery rat

and six lizards."

So, Cinderella fetched a pumpkin, six mice, a whiskery rat, and six lizards.

The fairy godmother touched
them with her wand…

and the pumpkin became a
golden coach,

the mice became six grey horses,

the rat became a coachman with
the most enormous moustache

and the lizards became six footmen
dressed in green and yellow.

Then, the fairy godmother
touched Cinderella with the
wand...

and her old dress became a golden
dress sparkling with jewels, while
on her feet was the prettiest pair of
glass slippers ever seen.

"Remember," said the fairy
godmother, "you must leave the
ball before the clock strikes twelve,
because at midnight the
magic ends."

"Thank you, fairy godmother,"
said Cinderella. And she climbed
into the coach.

When Cinderella arrived at the ball, she looked so beautiful that everyone wondered who she was.

Even the ugly sisters!

The prince asked her to dance with him, and they danced all evening.

He would not dance with anyone else.

Now, Cinderella was enjoying the ball so much that she forgot her fairy godmother's warning, until it was almost midnight and the clock began to strike.

One. Two. Three. She ran out of the ballroom.

Four. Five. Six. As she ran down the palace steps, one of her glass slippers fell off.

Seven. Eight. Nine. She ran towards the golden coach.

Ten. Eleven.

Twelve!

Then, there was Cinderella in
her old dress.

A pumpkin lay at her feet, and scampering down the road were six mice, a whiskery rat and six lizards.

So, Cinderella had to walk home, and by the time the ugly sisters returned, she was sweeping the floor!

Now, when Cinderella ran from the palace, the prince followed her, and he found the glass slipper.

He said, "I shall marry the beautiful girl whose foot fits this slipper."

In the morning, the prince went from house to house with the glass slipper, and every young lady tried to squeeze her foot into it. But it didn't fit any of them.

At last the prince came to Cinderella's house.

First one ugly sister tried to squash a foot into the slipper, but her foot was too big and fat.

Then the other ugly sister tried, but her foot was too long and thin.

"Please," said Cinderella, "let me try."

"The slipper won't fit you!" said the ugly sisters. "You didn't go to the ball!"

But Cinderella slipped her foot into the glass slipper, and it fitted perfectly.

Then – *WHOOSH!* Beside her stood the fairy godmother. She touched Cinderella with her wand…

and there she was in a golden dress sparkling with jewels, and on her feet was the prettiest pair of glass slippers ever seen.

The ugly sisters were so surprised.
They couldn't think of anything to
say!

But the prince knew what to
say – he asked Cinderella to
marry him.

And then there was a happy
wedding. Everyone who had
gone to the ball was invited –
even the ugly sisters! There was
wonderful food and lots of
music and dancing.

And the prince, of
course, danced every dance
with Cinderella.

FIRST FAIRY TALES
by Margaret Mayo
Illustrated by Philip Norman

Enjoy a little more magic with these First Fairy Tales:

❏ Cinderella	1 84121 150 8	£3.99
❏ Hansel and Gretel	1 84121 148 6	£3.99
❏ Jack and the Beanstalk	1 84121 146 X	£3.99
❏ Sleeping Beauty	1 84121 144 3	£3.99
❏ Rumpelstiltskin	1 84121 152 4	£3.99
❏ Snow White	1 84121 154 0	£3.99

Colour Crackers
by Rose Impey
Illustrated by Shoo Rayner

Have you read any Colour Crackers?

❏ A Birthday for Bluebell	1 84121 228 8	£3.99
❏ Hot Dog Harris	1 84121 232 6	£3.99
❏ Tiny Tim	1 84121 240 7	£3.99
❏ Too Many Babies	1 84121 242 3	£3.99

and many other titles.

First Fairy Tales and Colour Crackers are available from all good
bookshops, or can be ordered direct from the publisher:
Orchard Books, PO BOX 29, Douglas IM99 1BQ
Credit card orders please telephone 01624 836000
or fax 01624 837033
or e-mail: bookshop@enterprise.net for details.

To order please quote title, author and ISBN
and your full name and address.
Cheques and postal orders should be
made payable to 'Bookpost plc'.
Postage and packing is FREE within the UK
(overseas customers should add £1.00 per book).

Prices and availability are subject to change.